Way Far Away
on a
Wild Safari

by
Jan Peck

illustrated by
Valeria Petrone

SIMON & SCHUSTER BOOKS FOR YOUNG READERS
New York London Toronto Sydney

SIMON & SCHUSTER BOOKS FOR YOUNG READERS
An imprint of Simon & Schuster Children's Publishing Division
1230 Avenue of the Americas, New York, New York 10020
Text copyright © 2006 by Jan Peck

Illustrations copyright © 2006 by Valeria Petrone
Book design by Lucy Ruth Cummins
The text for this book is set in Fink Heavy.
The illustrations for this book are rendered digitally.
Manufactured in China
2 4 6 8 10 9 7 5 3
CIP data for this book is available from the Library of Congress.
ISBN-13: 978-1-4169-0072-6
ISBN-10: 1-4169-0072-1

With love to my family: Ken, Konrad, and Rohm—J. P.

To Carlo the King lion—V. P.

Way far away on a wild safari,
I'm hunting for a lion
for my grandma and me.
I'm so brave,
can't scare me,
way far away on a wild safari.

Way far away on a wild safari,
I spy an elephant spraying at me.
Hello, elephant.
Hose nose, elephant.
See you later, elephant.

Hike away.

Way far away on a wild safari,
I spy a giraffe standing TALL
   above me.
Hello, giraffe.
Your royal *highness*, giraffe.
See you later, giraffe.

Hike away.

Way far away on a wild safari,
I spy a hippopotamus sloshing by me.
Hello, hippopotamus.
Big bottom-a-mus, hippopotamus.
See you later, hippopotamus.

Hike away.

Way far away on a wild safari,
I spy a zebra zigzagging by me.
Hello, zebra.
Yikes! Stripes! Zebra.
See you later, zebra.

Hike away.

Way far away on a wild safari,
I spy a rhinoceros charging by me.
Hello, rhinoceros.
Whoa, whoa, rhinoceros!
See you later, rhinoceros.

Hike away.

Way far away on a wild safari,
I spy a gorilla spying on ME!
Hello, gorilla.
Thumbs-up, gorilla.
See you later, gorilla.

Hike away.

Way far away on a wild safari,
I spy a wildebeest snorting at me.
Hello, wildebeest.
What's gnu, wildebeest?
See you later, wildebeest.

Hike away.

Way far away on a wild safari,
I spy a hyena laughing at me.
Hello, hyena.
Fetch a funny bone, hyena?
See you later, hyena.

Hike away.

Way far away on a wild safari,
I spy an ostrich dancing by me.
Hello, ostrich.
Shake your feathers, ostrich.
See you later, ostrich.

Hike away.

Way far away on a wild safari,
I spy a lion ROARing at me!

Good-bye, lion!

Good-bye, ostrich.
Good-bye, hyena.
Good-bye, wildebeest.
Good-bye, gorilla.

Good-bye, rhinoceros.
Good-bye, zebra.
Good-bye, hippopotamus.
Good-bye, giraffe.
Good-bye, elephant.

Way back home from a wild safari,
I find Grandma waiting for me.
Hello, Grandma!
Guess what, Grandma?
I tamed a lion on a wild safari!